P9-DZM-338

Wish Upon A Star

Ariel Books
Andrews and McMeel
Kansas City

Wish Upon A Star

A Tale of Bedtime Magic

Armand Eisen
Illustrated by Robyn Officer

For Olivia Helprin
—AE

WISH UPON A STAR copyright © 1993 by Armand Eisen. All rights reserved. Printed in Hong Kong. No part of this book may be used or reproduced in any manner whatsoever without written permission except in the case of reprints in the context of reviews. For information write Andrews and McMeel, a Universal Press Syndicate Company, 4900 Main Street, Kansas City, Missouri 64112.

Library of Congress Catalog Card Number: 93-70499

ISBN: 0-8362-4937-2

Design: Diane Stevenson / Snap-Haus Graphics

Wish Upon A Star

Olivia wasn't at all tired. But her mother kissed her on the cheek and said, "Now, it's bedtime, dear. Turn off the lights and have sweet dreams."

"Why do I have to go to sleep?" Olivia said with a big yawn. "The stars don't turn off their lights. They get to stay up and play all night long. I wish *I* could play with them. I wish...I wish...I wish...."

Olivia's head sunk into her nice soft feather pillow. She yawned again and her heavy eyelids closed. "I wish...I wish...I wish..." she thought as she drifted away.

Olivia fell into a beautiful sleep—she felt as though she were floating on air.

She felt as light as the summer wind
that blows the clouds across the sky.

"Dear me!" said Olivia, as she opened her eyes, "I am flying way up in the sky!"

"Have fun, Olivia," a friendly cloud called out to her.

"I will," said Olivia, as she drifted higher and higher.

"Hello and welcome, Olivia!" said the brightest star she had ever seen. "Would you like to stay up all night and play with us?"

"Oh, yes!" said Olivia.

"How about a ride on my rings?" asked Saturn.
"Oh, may I? What fun!" said Olivia.

"I think you need a rest," called out the Man in the Moon. "Come over here and sit down for a while."

"Why, thank you very much," said Olivia, "but only for a minute, because there is so much to see."

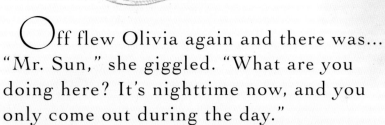

Off flew Olivia again and there was...
"Mr. Sun," she giggled. "What are you
doing here? It's nighttime now, and you
only come out during the day."

"You have been playing up here longer
than you think," said Mr. Sun. "It's almost
morning and time for you to say goodbye."

"Goodbye, Star," she said. "Thank you for all the fun."

"Goodbye, Olivia," replied the Star. "Here's a little gift to wear to remind you of my friends and me."

"Oh, thank you," said Olivia, as she felt a little tingle around her wrist.

"Oh, my! It's almost daylight! I better fly
home as fast as I can!" Olivia cried.
And in the time it takes to blink your eyes...

...Olivia found herself in her very own bed. "What a wonderful dream," she thought. "It seemed so real—like it wasn't a dream at all."